Look Out, Kindergarten, Here I Come!

by Nancy Carlson

¡Prepárate, kindergarten! ¡Allá voy!

Por Nancy Carlson

VIKING

VIKING
Published by Penguin Group
Penguin Young Readers Group, 345 Hudson Street, New York, New York 10014, U.S.A.
Penguin Books Ltd, 80 Strand, London WC2R 0RL, England
Penguin Books Australia Ltd, 250 Camberwell Road, Camberwell, Victoria 3124, Australia
Penguin Books Canada Ltd, 10 Alcorn Avenue, Toronto, Ontario, Canada M4V 3B2
Penguin Books (N.Z.) Ltd, 182-190 Wairau Road, Auckland 10, New Zealand

English edition published in 1999 by Viking, a division of Penguin Putnam Books for Young Readers.
This bilingual edition published in 2004 by Viking, a division of Penguin Young Readers Group.

25

Copyright © Nancy Carlson, 1999
Translation copyright © Penguin Group (USA) Inc., 2004
All rights reserved
Translated by Teresa Mlawer

The Library of Congress has cataloged the English edition as follows:
Carlson, Nancy L.
Look out, kindergarten, here I come! / Nancy Carlson.
p   cm.
Summary: Even though Henry is looking forward to going to kindergarten, he is not sure about staying once he first gets there.
ISBN: 0-670-88378-6
[1. Kindergarten—Fiction. 2. First day of school—Fiction.]
I. Title.
PZ7.C21665Lim 1999 [E]—dc21 98-47039 CIP AC

This edition ISBN: 978-0-670-03673-8

Manufactured in China
Set in Avenir

To Maureen Beck—a dedicated educator who helped
me come up with the idea for this book.

A Maureen Beck, una educadora dedicada, quien
me sugirió la idea de este libro.

"Wake up, dear," said Henry's mom. "It's the first day of kindergarten."

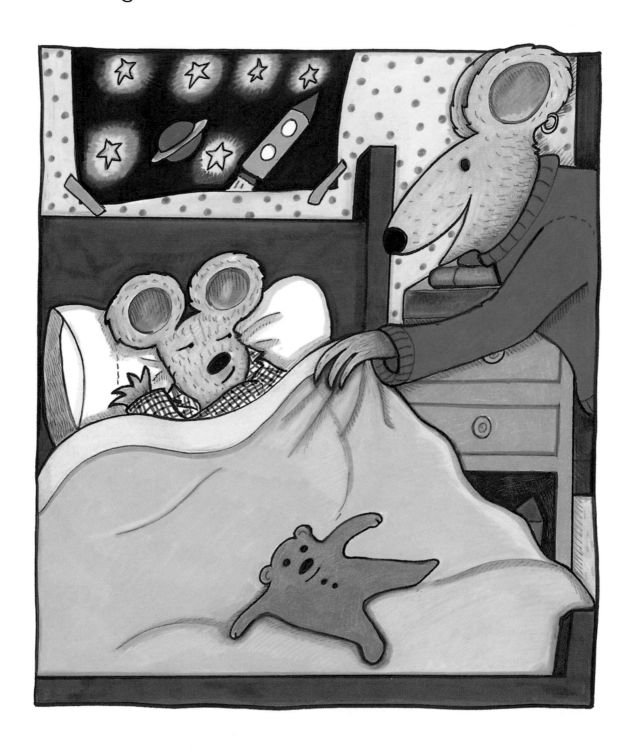

—Despierta, cariño —dijo la mamá de Henry—.
¡Ha llegado el día! Te espera el kindergarten.

"Oh boy! Let's go!" said Henry. He had been getting ready for this day all year.
"Not so fast," said his mom. "First you need to wash up and get dressed."

—¡Qué bien! ¡Vámonos ya! —saltó Henry. Había estado esperando este día durante todo el año.
—Espera... —le dijo su mamá—. Primero tienes que lavarte y vestirte.

So Henry brushed his teeth the way his dentist had shown him and washed behind his ears.

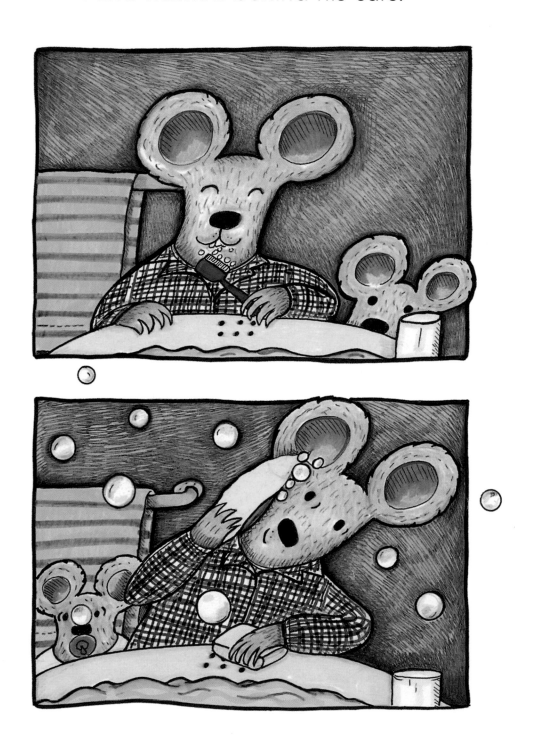

Henry se cepilló los dientes como le había enseñado el dentista y se lavó detrás de las orejas.

Then he buttoned his shirt and snapped his jeans and *almost* tied his shoes.

Después se abotonó la camisa, se puso los vaqueros y *casi* consiguió atarse él solo los cordones de los zapatos.

"Okay, I'm all ready for kindergarten!" said Henry. "Not so fast," said his mom. "First you need a good breakfast."

—Bueno, ¡ya estoy listo para ir al kindergarten! —dijo Henry. —Espera... —le dijo su mamá—. Antes tienes que desayunar.

So Henry ate three pancakes and a bowl of fruit and drank a big glass of milk.

Henry se comió tres panqueques y un plato de frutas, y se bebió un vaso de leche.

"Now I'm ready to go!" said Henry.
"Not so fast," said his mom. "You still need to pack up your supplies."

—¡Ya está! —dijo Henry.
—Espera . . . —respondió su mamá—. Todavía tienes que preparar tus cosas.

So Henry packed pencils, scissors, crayons, paper, glue, an apple, and . . .

Henry metió en la mochila lápices, tijeras, crayolas, papel, pegamento, una manzana, y . . .

a photo of his mom and dad
(in case he got lonely).

una foto de mamá y papá
(por si se sentía solo).

"Now I'm ready!"
said Henry.

—¡Ahora sí que estoy listo!
—dijo Henry.

"What do you think we'll do first?" asked Henry.
"Do you think we'll paint?"

—¿Qué crees que haremos primero? —preguntó Henry—.
¿Dibujar?

"Sure you will," said his mom. "Just like at home."
"Good!" said Henry. "What else will we do?"

—Sí, claro —le respondió su mamá—. Como hacemos en casa.
—¡Qué bien! —dijo Henry—. ¿Y qué más?

"You'll probably learn your ABC's," said his mom.

—Seguro que te enseñan el abecedario —dijo su mamá.

"Hey, I already know the letters in my name!" said Henry. "What will we do after that?"

—Ya me sé las letras de mi nombre —respondió Henry—. ¿Y qué haremos después?

"You'll sing songs,

—Cantarán canciones,

and play games,

jugarán,

and you might practice counting," said his mom.

y aprenderán a contar —dijo su mamá.

"One, two, three flowers," said Henry. "I can count to ten, because we practiced counting with buttons. What comes next?"

—Una, dos, tres flores —dijo Henry—. Sé contar hasta diez, porque practicamos contando botones. ¿Y después qué haremos?

"You'll make fun things in arts and crafts, and you'll read stories."

—Divertidas manualidades . . . Y leerán cuentos.

"But I can't read!" said Henry.
"That's okay," said his mom. "You'll start by listening. Reading comes later."

—Pero yo no sé leer —dijo Henry.
—No te preocupes —le dijo su mamá—. Primero escucharás y luego aprenderás.

"Here we are," said Henry's mom.
"It's so *big*," said Henry. "What if I get lost?"

—Ya hemos llegado —dijo la mamá de Henry.
—¡Qué grande es! —exclamó Henry—. ¿Y si me pierdo?

"Remember, we found your room and your cubby at Kindergarten Roundup," said his mom. "But you can always ask a teacher for help."

—Recuerda que encontramos tu clase y tu casillero el día que vinimos de visita —dijo su mamá—. Pero siempre puedes pedirle ayuda a algún maestro.

When Henry got to his room and saw
lots of new faces, he said,

Cuando Henry llegó a su clase y vio tantas
caras nuevas, dijo:

"I want to go home!"

—¡Quiero irme a casa!

"Why don't you come in and look around?" said his teacher, Ms. Bradley.

—¿Por qué no entras un momento? —le dijo su maestra, la señorita Bradley.

So Henry looked around. He saw the art corner.
He saw letters and numbers that he knew.

Henry miró a su alrededor. Vio que había un rincón para
pintar. También vio letras y números que conocía . . .

He saw a bookcase full of books, and he met a new friend to play with.

. . . Una estantería llena de libros y encontró a una amiga con quien jugar.

"Well, what do you think?" asked Henry's mom.
"I think I might stay for a while, Mom," said Henry,

—Bueno, ¿qué te parece? —le preguntó su mamá.
—Creo que me quedaré un rato, mamá —dijo Henry.

"because kindergarten is going to be fun!"

¡El kindergarten va a ser muy divertido!